Dangerous Vanity

Dr. Sharon Campbell-Phillips

ISBN 978-93-5610-787-8

Published in India 2022 by Pencil

A brand of
One Point Six Technologies Pvt. Ltd.
123, Building J2, Shram Seva Premises,
Wadala Truck Terminal, Wadala (E)
Mumbai 400037, Maharashtra, INDIA
E connect@thepencilapp.com
W www.thepencilapp.com

Author biography

My name is Dr. Sharon Campbell-Phillips. I am from Trinidad and Tobago. I am very enthusiastic about community work and the development of others. I am also very passionate about conducting research and writing as it allows me the opportunity to share my knowledge with others and educate them as well as enhance and develop myself.

I am currently employed with the local government of Trinidad and Tobago where I work in the Division of Community Development. This Division is dedicated to developing communities so that persons' standard of living can be enhanced.

My writing career began when I was approached by a classmate from Bangladesh to collaborate and write professionally. I accepted the challenge and we began writing together. When I received my first publication, I was very excited and was motivated to continue writing, I am also a Doctor of Health Sciences. My passion for writing allows me to complete individual projects, as well as collaborate with others to produce impressive work.

Phone: +1868 7511022

Email: sharoncampbell433@gmail.com

CONTENTS

Chapter One

Amari Camden is an executed Barbadian doctor. He grew up not bad but his mother regularly struggled to make ends meet. She got so frustrated at one factor she might convey guys home while her concept Amari become asleep and they might pay her to have intercourse. The bills were continually paid now and meals were continually in the house and he got a greater allowance.

Amari got up one night to visit the restroom and the noises he heard coming from his mother's bedroom excited him. A budding youngster with a brand new observed hobby, he was destined for the hassle. When Amari's mother wasn't at home, he might drill a small hole into the wooden wall of her bedroom from his. He made certain he amassed all the dirt and washed it down the sink. His mom's mattress turned into some distance aspect of her bedroom far away from the wall so irrespective of where he positioned the hollow he could have an extraordinary view of what become going on. Sure enough, late at night time, he might flip the light off in his room and he could pay attention to voices bypassing his bedroom. Minutes later he might flow the picture and take a glance. What Amari saw the first night time extra than excited him. He got so aroused he felt like crying due to the fact he failed to understand how to make his erection go down.

Every night time for the subsequent four years it might be the same thing. Late at night, his mom would deliver home the men. Amari in no way had to move anywhere to find out about what to do with the mattress, he learned it properly at domestic.

One day his mother changed into rearranging her room and she or he determined the hollow. She went into Amari's room and attempted to determine where it might be. She moved each picture and whilst she saw it, her coronary heart broke. She constantly idea she turned into cautious but simplest now she knew the ramifications of her moves. Amari changed into now 17 and he desired to be a medical doctor and they might let nothing prevent him from achieving this. When he got home from school that day, his mother sat him down.

"What's up mother?" "How lengthy have you been looking at me, Amari? Amari couldn't find a crater anywhere to fall into.

"I by no means wanted you to peer me like that. It's not how matters are purported to be and I do not want you to treat girls that way either. Be the best at the whole lot you do but deal with women with recognizing do you listen to me?"

"Yes, mum." Amari held onto his mother for what appeared like an hour. He didn't even recognize she had stopped respiration because he had fallen asleep.

"Mom? MOM?"

He ran to the neighbor's residence and shortly all of us turned frantic, the police got there the ambulance, and the coroner. Amari stayed in his bedroom. What could he do now? How is he going to stay in college? He knew of no circle of relatives he should live with.

One of his neighbors knocked at the bedroom door.

"Amari, have you eaten because you got here home?" "No sir." "Come, my spouse cooked, let's get you fed and we can talk approximately your subsequent steps.

Amari got up, took the keys from the wall, and locked the door at the back of him.

He changed into sitting at the desk eating and a young woman he was sweet on came into the room.

"Hi Amari, sorry to hear about your mom, she became so exceptional to me." "Thank you." She sat down next to him and took his hand. "It could be ok Dad will find out what you are going to do and the rest folks will pitch in wherein we will."

"Okay thank you." He persisted consuming seeking to forget about the annoyance among his legs. He scooted further underneath the chair to keep away from being seen. Over the next few days, all and sundry helped Amari out. They delivered him food and helped out with the payments. He was given a process working so he ought to assist himself as correctly.

The female round the corner would sneak into his room and they might spend the time they'd kissing and fondling each different. They were both too scared to move any further and as time went by using they have been content to play with every different body.

One day he had just come home and a man changed into sitting on the front porch. "Can I assist you, sir?" "I'm right here representing your mother as her lawyer. Can we cross inner that is a non-public remember?" "Sure."

Amari took his keys out, opened the door, and allow the man in. "Have a seat might you want something to drink?" "Something with bubbles could be nice." Amari took a Sprite from the fridge and took it to the gentleman. He opened it took a sip and closed his eyes.

"That became what I needed, thank you. Now down to business. My call is Fredrique Bynoe and I am right here to deliver letters out of your mom's property. These are yours for starters and you could signal here that you have obtained them sealed and intact." He handed Amari four envelopes and a shape to signal.

"Now, I have bank account information and college files as properly, you want to sign for the ones as nicely." He passed him an envelope from a financial institution and one from the university his mother had picked out for him. He signed and surpassed lower back that form.

"Now the best part. Your mom advised me what she had been doing for the remaining 5 years or so. I understand you might imagine badly of her but she changed into a very good lady and she did the entirety she had to due to the fact she wanted you to succeed in life. She asked me to make a few investments for her and that they paid off, I just desire she were here to peer it. These my son are yours."

Mr. Bynoe passed Amari four documents. There have been statements from four organizations he had invested money for his mother. Over three hundred and fifty thousand dollars in all. The statement from the financial

institution said eight thousand dollars and the Credit union also had approximately eight thousand dollars, which one became for financial savings best.
"How did my mom do all of this?" "I can handiest let you know that she in no way intended to do that for the relaxation of her lifestyle, she turned into saving sufficient cash to send you to college, and then you definitely might do the rest. She decided she would not cheapen herself similarly and best chose a successful business guy, at the least that way she knew she should get the right coins. Son, you don't need the info, she did the satisfactorily she should. Now your college expenses are paid incomplete. The mortgage on the residence is paid in full as nicely and it's for your name. Sign right here and right here."
Mr. Bynoe marked the regions along with his pen. Amari was shocked, all of the time he turned into watching his mother degrade herself, and she turned into creating a way for him. The papers stated he changed to start school in some months and it wasn't too far. He should experience his motorcycle there and back. "Now closing however now not least. Everything your mother left is yours, a number of it you may get now and the relaxation you could best get admission to whilst you end your studies. The financial institution account is yours to use as you notice in shape, like a bonus. Your credit score union account is for use for deposits simplest. Your mom counseled that you use it for emergencies best. The dividends from the investments will gather and whilst you get your name they become yours. I gained make investments anymore except you assert so and no I don't have any real get right of entry to the money, so no worry of it disappearing. Do you understand everything to

date?" "Yes sir. I'm nonetheless in shock. I will do my mother proud."

"I'm positive you'll son. Now, this is my card, if you want any help call me day or night. I should move now, my office is about fifteen minutes from right here so you can pop in and let me realize how you are doing." "Thank you sir bye now." Amari sat down and cried his eyes out.

Chapter Two

Three months later, he started out reading to be a physician. He was careful with his money. He did not go out consuming or partying, he turned continually to his books. The reminiscences of his mother's escapades at night gradually dimmed in his mind and he remembered simplest the good and wonderful matters approximately her.

Amari spent the next ten years assembly every standard, he passed each exam with almost ideal rankings. He couldn't make up his thoughts if he desired to open a sanatorium or paintings in a health facility. He selected each. He took half of the money from his investment account and purchased a construction in Belleville. Where maximum of the medical doctors in Barbados flows into. He got all his licenses and files organized and in about six months he became geared up. He was now a qualified Orthopedic Surgeon.

Amari became now thirty years of age and apart from losing his virginity at twenty-one, he had no longer been inquisitive about a female friend or even sex until he saw a female sitting on a step in tears. He stopped his car and got out.

"Miss, can I help? Are you ill?" "No, I'm about to be evicted from my home." She handed him the notice and he or she had approximately three weeks. "Do you have a

process?" "No the company near down that's why I haven't been able to pay my lease." "I have an opening as a cleaner, you can have it in case you want."
"I could as a substitute die than be a maid. I have something else in my thoughts. You look like a single man, how approximately I provide you with all the sex you need, and also you pay my rent every month for the time we're collective." Amari stepped again. His notion he turned into helping a damsel in misery but she turned out to be a whore in cover. "No thank you, correct luck together with your lease."
"What you think you are too proper for me is that it? I will have you recognize I even have a degree in Business Management, I've in no way done drugs and I've had this apartment for six years. Two months" lease and they're throwing me out. I'm not inquisitive about a boyfriend proper now and my offer would suit us both. You may not need to fear approximately me sleeping with different men, due to the fact I don't sleep around. Look overlook it. Have a very good evening."
"Why might you advocate one of these elements, I am a stranger to you." "You stopped to look if you could help, do you have any concept of what that announces about you?" "I see. Tell you what. Have dinner with me and could discover a manner to clear up your trouble without you promoting yourself to me for hire cash." "Okay allow me to move to change. Come on in."
Amar remotely locked his vehicle and accompanied the lady internal. The apartment turned into properly furnished and tidy. She disappeared right into a room and when she got here back she seemed absolutely one-of-a-kind. "Wow, your appearance is brilliant. What is your

call?"

"Alayna Jones, yours?"

"Amari Camden."

"Nice to meet you, we could?"

Amari confirmed Alayna to his vehicle, she didn't fuss over the fact that he drove the 2014 Acura MDX. He could see she favored it and was puzzled why she did not remark. He turned glad at first due to the fact if she did he might assume she turned into going out with him for his money. That didn't remain lengthy. "Nice vehicle, how a good deal did you pay for it?" "Why does that matter?" "An automobile tells the entirety about its proprietor." "The automobile not the rate. Doctors need to paintings for a dwelling, I labored for this automobile, think nothing of it." "Oh, sorry."

They talked about little things, likes, dislikes, and what they desired from a date. Amari turned into starting to see the sort of person Alayna become and he changed into not liking it in any respect. She appeared enthusiastic about money and whilst he pulled as much as the restaurant, he may want to see the celebrities in her eyes. To him, it became just some other luxurious location to eat.

Alayna ordered, the most high-priced matters on the menu and she didn't even consume all. Amari had had sufficient of her and he desired the nighttime to be over. When he drove as much as her building, he got out, opened her door, and helped her out.

"Come on up Amari, you already know you need to." She walked away, unlocked the door, and left it open. Amari hesitated at the beginning but what did he ought to lose? A night of a laugh and he might also by no means see her again. When he was given to her bedroom door, Alayna become already bare and sprawled throughout her bed. Amari stripped, put on a condom, and went over to her.

Amari changed into now not an accomplished lover, he barely knew what to do and Alayna regarded him as though she knew the whole lot so he just allows her to have her amusing. When they were finished Amari got up and commenced to dress.

"So, are you going to assist me with the hire?"

"How tons is it?"

"Eight hundred dollars for the two months."

"I do not have that on me, come by using the hospital the following day and acquire it."

"Okay. See you the day after today then. It became first-rate."

"Yes, it became."

Amari finished dressing and left in a bit of a rush. He felt as though he desired to throw up.

The next day he turned into sitting in his workplace making ready for the following patient and his Secretary buzzed and say Miss Alayna Jones changed into here to look him and he started to ship her in.

"Morning Amari."

"Morning Alayna." He exceeded her an envelope with the money.

"Thanks, will I see you again tonight?"

"Why to extract any other eight hundred dollars from me for an hour of sex? I do not suppose so. If this is the life you want to live, go do it with someone else. Have an excellent day." Alayna appeared shocked, she simply concept she could be residing excessively at the hog off the physician, boy turned into she incorrect. "You simply used to me to get intercourse, the least you can do changed into supplying me a touch bit extra cash."

"I gave you enough to pay your rent for three months and buy a few meals, now kindly go away from my office and do not come returned."

Alayna's face registered even greater shock. "Amari, I'm sorry I......"

"Don't. Just go away." He went lower back to his paperwork and omitted her completely. Alayna hung her head and left the health center. Amari felt terrible however he did not want that sort of lifestyle. As the months handed he labored tough on the health facility, he wanted to take a vacation so he hired another health practitioner to paint for the time he became away.

He had been looking into any other enterprise and it changed over time he made his move. He failed to expect the following couple of months in his lifestyle to play out as they did however matters take place and we simply must roll with the punches or get stuck up within the melee.

Amari wanted to get into real property, he had seen some town residences on Maxwell Main road, and he parent he ought to buy them and hire them out to travelers with families, it'd be lots inexpensive than a motel room. He additionally saw some vintage houses he wanted to shop for and attach up and both promote them or rent them out as nicely. He regarded via the newspapers and he noticed quite a few on the market. He referred to the numbers separately and by way of the stop of the week, he could be purchasing ten house coins. When he spoke to the proprietors, they had been currently evicting a few families and Amari did not like that one bit. He stored going returned to his mom and all she had to do for them to continue to exist. He said he might visit the households and try and figure out how he should help them get lower back on their feet.

The first residence he went to go to turned into a person with a spouse and children. Henry a creation employee and Juanne changed into a stay at domestic moms. The youngsters were both below ten years vintage. Amari had all recognized the husband however as soon as the spouse noticed his vehicle pull up, she did the whole thing she could to seduce him. Amari couldn't trust the danger this lady turned into taking to maintain her household collectively. She provided him something bloodless to drink while he first arrived and she or he hinted she changed into so warm that she wanted something to chill her down. When asked in which her husband became she instructed him he became at work but he ought to inform her something he desired to. She went into the kitchen and was given a drink and when she got here back her shirt became undone and her cleavage become displaying.

"If you want me simply say it, I could do something to hold a roof over my own family's head. I promise I won't move to blab to my friends, that won't do for either folk, simply don't tell my husband I did this." Amari looked at this first-class-looking girl who became willing to sleep with a rich man in place of growing to be in the streets and it changed into as though a mild in him went off.

"Two matters and neither of them is up for debate. You will not be sleeping with everybody else except me or your husband, we can now not do this indefinitely, I will talk to your husband and we can work out a plan to get your rent paid. You will arise off your lazy ass and find a process. I decide after I see you and if I ever listen about this from all

of us you will be sorry. Are we clean?"
All of a surprising Juanne became afraid of the person standing before her. She couldn't even talk, she just nodded her head. "This is my cope with, come tomorrow afternoon around lunchtime." Amari grew to become and left the residence. His heart changed into thumping in his chest. He knew what he changed into doing changed into wrong but he turned into starting to realize the electricity he had over women and he might use it pass get what he wanted, on every occasion he wanted.

Chapter Three

He had ten homes to visit and a pair more of them had other halves who were willing to sleep with him to save their houses. He decided to go away from the others for another time as he turned into presupposed to be on holiday and sex with three extraordinary women changed into sufficient for now. This went on for about three months. The health practitioner he hired at the medical institution decided it became higher surroundings for him and he determined to live on if Amari agreed. They labored out payment and it turned out to go smoothly. Amari had time to try different initiatives in his spare time.

With seven extra homes to go to, he commenced once more to see what sweets he could discover. After the ninth house and no good fortune, he turned prepared to give up. He checked the cope of the final residence and it was in a cul-de-sac and the closet residence changed into over three hundred feet away. The belongings turned into run down and he should handiest think of knocking it down and constructing a new one. He walked as much as the porch and knocked at the door. He was unprepared for the beauty that got here to the door. She was wearing a gentle button-down, yellow jersey dress that molded her parent. Her herbal braids have been piled on top of her head however he could see they had been at the least

shoulder period. Her eyes have been the most adorable shade of brown he had ever visible, her darkish pores and skin glowed as if she have been within the sun for hours.
"Good afternoon, my name is Dr. Camden and I…" He saw the girl step lower back and tears shaped in her eyes.
"We must leave now?"
"Leave now? Wait, no, I'm sorry to permit me to explain myself, can I come in and sit down for a minute?"
"Um, it is no longer the exceptional however it's all we've, if you could find a suitable chair, sit down at your very own danger." Amari found a barstool and sat on it. "I even have, Kool-Aid, lemonade, and mauby." "Mauby." She dropped some ice cubes in a tall glass and poured the drink into it.
Amari took it and stated thank you. When he took the first sip, he closed his eyes and moaned. "Sorry, it is not from the bottle, I make it from scratch with the bark."
"Oh this is extraordinary, I haven't had old skool mauby in years." "You are maximum welcome. The preceding landlord told about you shopping for the belongings. Now if you are not right here to evict us, why are you right here?" "This is the remaining one on my listing and I'm not right here to evict you. What I would love to do is restore the region up and paintings with you to find a manner to buy it for yourselves. How many of you live here?"
"Four, two children, my husband and myself. The kids are at college and my husband is out inside the lower back taking care of the vegetables." "Can you ask him to be available please, he wishes to pay attention to this as properly?" "Sure, deliver me a minute." She went out to the kitchen and Amari heard her name for a person.

About five minutes later she came again in with an unkempt and dirty man in tow.

"What do you need?" Immediately Amari disliked the man and wondered how he ended up with this kind of adorable spouse. "I'm right here to work out an agreement for the residence. I plan to restore it up and set up a lease to own." "Is that proper? I do not see how that's viable when we slightly got enough now, how the hell do you assume me to shop for a new house?"

Amari became shocked. How should this cute splendor likely be married to this oaf? He decided to take a danger.

"You could supply me your spouse in trade for the new residence." The lady looked up at Amari as though he had long past mad. "I'm no longer on the market." "How plenty we talking?" "This house is worth nothing, the brand new one can be worth at the least three hundred and fifty thousand dollars."

"Can we get the cash as opposed to the house?" "Sure however you'll have to discover a few locations to stay because the belongings remain mine and I would be losing twice on the deal."

"She is a satisfactory piece of ass, you can have her. The children stay with me." "Done. You can pile together with your luggage and be equipped in an hour." "I am NOT for sale and I am NOT leaving the children. This is unlawful, you can't do that to me. It's 2022 for crying out loud."

"I guess he lives in a few fancy residences and simply takes a look at the automobile he has too. Even his shoes are well worth more than this residence. Think of the matters we can buy the kids sooner or later. We don't need you right here proper now anyway. I will assist you percent. "I am now not going everywhere." "Yes you're, you may come to see the kids anytime you want. Do this for them, you comprehend it's the proper component to do."

"I can't accept as true this. After all, I've performed for you that is the way you treat me? Fine!! Dr. Camden, I could be equipped whilst you get back. She grew to become and left the two men. "What a bitch." "If I ever hear you talk to her in any derogatory names once more you might not get another cent from me. I can be lower back in an hour with your cheque. What call shall I put it in?" "Justin Forde." "Fine. See then you."

Chapter Four

Amari drove away with a heat feeling in his stomach. He may want to see the hurt inside the female's eyes however he may also see a degree of alleviation. He desired her to convey the children however he needed some time with her first. She wasn't like the other halves he has been seeing. She became a fighter and even though she had given in to her husband's bullying, he knew she could not deliver it to him so effortlessly. He might have to tug out every prevention in convincing her that her life would be higher off with him after which he would deliver the children as properly.

An hour later Amari show up at the Forde house with a cheque for $350 thousand greenbacks. Caitlin is sitting on the front porch with suitcases and a handbag in her lap. She looks as if a person knock the wind out of her and there was a mark on her cheek.

"Did he hurt you, Mrs. Forde?" She seemed up at Amari and the tears fell. Amari very well pushed the front door and went inside and before Justin should react Amari punched him inside the face and knocked him returned about four feet. He flung the cheque at him and left. Caitlin changed into already sitting in his automobile whilst he got here out. He got in and drove away. "What's your call?" "Caitlin." "I even have a proposal for you Caitlin."

"What's that? You're going to pay Justin every other three

hundred and fifty to sleep with me?" "No, I would love permission to take you on a date," Amaris spoke softly. "A date?" Caitlin's shock registered in her voice. "Yes, a date. When turned into the closing time you went out and had some clean a laugh?"

"Never! I married Justin when I was twenty, then the children showed up." "Say sure and I will take you out, no strings." "Are you severe?" Caitlin's eyes lit up. "Very." "I..........." She was about to mention she didn't have anything to wear. "I would also want to take you purchasing." "Can we get a few stuff for the kids?" "I just paid your husband, he can get things for the youngsters." "They gained see a cent of that cash, Dr. Camden. I'm the one who looks after them twenty-four hours an afternoon. Since Justin added them home he has never paid any interest to them, they are going to be so unhappy after they get domestic. Can they arrive over for visits?"

"Anything to thrill you." "Why me? You ought to have any woman you want." "You grew to become me down. I've visited ten homes and you are the only wife who has become me down."

"Are you still seeing them?" She requested before she should forestall herself. "After these days no longer a danger. Wait what do you suggest bringing them home? The kids aren't yours?"

"No, my husband cheated on me with separate ladies on the night of our wedding six years in the past, each child is five years of age. I have no for Justin, nor do I wish to." "I see. I'm sorry you had to go through that. Where would love to go shopping?" "You are asking me? I have in no way shopped for clothes in my lifestyle, all of the clothes I introduced with me from domestic I nonetheless

have. We never had any money for exceptional matters and anything we make from the garden I ensure the kids get to school and have something to devour. You made a poor choice Dr. Camden."
"I beg to vary, every so often we make selections however we don't see our efforts for a protracted whilst. I will have someone come to the residence and you could choose out what you want first, then as time passes you will have your very own money and you can shop on your own, honest sufficient?" "How long do you intend to maintain me?"
"Honestly you are not a prisoner, if you decided you wanted to head back domestic, I could take you and find a manner so one can get the residence legally." "Okay, will you.........?

"No Caitlin, I do not assume you to have intercourse with me, although that was my unique intention. You are a very lovely female." Caitlin bowed her head. When they pulled as much as Amari's house Caitlin, blinked for a few seconds, she expected something one-of-a-kind. Sure the house turned huge but it looked like someone simply lived there and it wasn't only for display. There were fruit trees inside the lawn, a pleasant manicured lawn, and a small fountain and there was flora all over the place, there has been a love swing beneath a mango tree and what looked to her like a fish pond. Amari was given out and opened her door. When he held out his hand, she hesitated. Then she took it and stepped out. They walked up to the residence and Amari unlocked the door and stepped in.
"Welcome to my home." "Oh Dr. Camden this is cute, you stay right here on my own?" "Well now that you are right here no and my name is Amari. Would you want

something to drink?" "Yes please." "The kitchen is that way, help yourself, this is your own home now as nicely." Amari went returned to the auto and took her suitcases out. He contemplated giving her rcom however he wanted to feel her body after him at night time, even supposing they failed to make love. Caitlin was special and he could do the whole thing he should to make her experience snug.

When he got here again from the bedroom, Caitlin became cooking. "Caitlin?" "Sorry, I didn't understand in case you had eaten and I idea I could put together something for you. Today has been an unexpected one and I am not positive what you need of me." "What I need is which will experience at domestic, you aren't my maid or slave, you're free to return and pass as you please. Let me provide you with a warning even though. I will provide it my first-rate shot at seeking to make you go away from your husband. I will never force you to do something you do not need to, apprehend me?"

"Yes, Amari. We don't have a telephone at domestic, can you take me to the lower back to see the kids, I want to inform them I received be there for them for some time, as a minimum till I get settled here." "You love them that tons?"

"Oh I had no choice, they're the excellent factor to appear to me, and they provide me a lot of pleasure. I knew nothing approximately elevating kids, I became a simplest toddler and..........." "Go on." He stated softly. "My father became terrible and he made my mom prostitute herself to feed the family, while Justin came along he changed into rich just like you, and they gave me to him. I idea I could have had a better life, however, he became really under the influence of alcohol and a gambler and inside a year anything cash he had amassed, become long gone. We were given this residence lease unfastened for a year because it became antique. I started the lawn and I give the former owner several of what I grew and that's what has been maintaining us afloat. Justin brought domestic Catherine first, she turned into only some weeks' old, quiet little issue. He sold home Joshua a twelve months later it changed into then I found out after they might have been conceived. He blatantly confessed everything. Fortunately, he became too drunk to consummate our marriage, and I by no means allow him to touch me. I raised those youngsters as my own and if something came about to them due to me, I would die."

"Tell you what, they can come for visits on weekends however you can pass and see them whenever you want although." "Thank you, they would love it right here, especially the pool, I might need to get them a few floatation gadgets though, they cannot swim but." "Not a trouble, I can educate them, provide me a minute will you?" "Sure." Caitlin persisted in cooking. She heard Amari speaking on his cell smartphone. When he changed into finished he got here back into the kitchen.

"The non-public client could be right here later this nighttime. I have a question for you." "Would you want to have children of your personal?" "I'm no longer sure if I can, I've by no means been to peer a medical doctor earlier than." "You want to get complete checkup honey. Tell you what, visit my medical institution and feature the whole lot achieved, I will cover the prices." "Your belonging to a health facility?" "Yes, I do." "Oh." "That smells first-class.' "Thank you, it will be finished soon." She became again to the range and she or he should sense Amari looking at her. "Caitlin?" She turned to stand him again. "I'm no longer positive what I am doing here, I have made many errors with women inside the last few months and I need to inform you something." "Are you going to hurt me?" "No. I would never do that." "Are you an assassin?" "No." "Are you a rapist?" "Not in that experience of the phrase no. Let me finish." "My mom bought herself to men to hold us fed. When she died, all of the money she made sent me to college, paid for our house, and an entire set of other matters. I cherished and hated her for an extended even as. I sold some residences and after I first started out going to the families to speak to them, I ended up bargaining with the wives for intercourse. It went on for approximately three months or so. When I saw you I had the same deal in mind however while you said no, it did something to me. The three wives had no remorse by any means in napping with me. You then again informed me flat out no, even though you and Justin have the arena of issues and I even have the maximum admiration for you. Honestly, given that assembly, several things have taken place. I am determined to disengage myself from the women, I would like to create a loving home for you so you might not want to go away. I would like to satisfy the children soon and see how I can assist them as nicely and final however not least. I even have never met a lady who I notion I will be married to till these days. I recognize this is a lot to absorb and prefer I stated you aren't a prisoner however I would love you to strive for a relationship with me and spot how it goes."

Caitlin became off the stove and turned to stand Amari. She walked over to him and stood close.

"Kiss me, Amari." Amari failed to falter, he took her face in his palms, and whilst his lips touched hers, a planet somewhere exploded. Her lips have been soft and heat and she smelt like golden apples. Caitlin moaned and unfolded for Amari. He deepened the kiss and his fingers left her face and moved to her waist. He knew she turned into getting aroused, her body language became giving off all the signs. She positioned her hands around his neck and leaned into him.

"Caitlin........." He pulled back and checked out her. He breasts have been growing and falling, her pores and skin glowed even extra now and her eyes have been closed. Just then a tear trickled down her cheek. "What's incorrect honey, am I moving too fast?" "Justin by no means kissed me like that. No one has ever kissed me like that." "It's ok, we can forestall now or I might not be capable of departing you alone." "Am I turning you off?" "Open your eyes, honey."

Caitlin opened her eyes and whilst she noticed Amari's personal, she ought to see the preference staring returned at her. "I'm taking a danger right here. Don't be afraid." He pulled her near once more and this time he permit her to experience his erection against her hip. "I do not recognize Amari." "Have you by no means been held near like this earlier than?" "No, the guy has ever touched me, no longer even Justin."

Amari was blown away. He knew she become unique but this was extra than he ever imagined. "Honey, I promise you this, if you decide to stay with me I will keep you want this each day so long as you allow me. Now, I need to assist you to go due to the fact after that confession I would like to take you to a mattress and make love to you all day." "I need you to Amari." "Not but honey, we've got lots of time. We get to understand each other and while it occurs, we might not have any doubts or regrets, understood?" "Yes." "Now how old are you?" "Twenty-six. You?" "Thirty-seven."

"Come on let's devour. What time will the youngsters be domestic?" "The bus will drop them off around 3:15." "Okay, we will get there earlier than then." They sat at the breakfast desk and ate and talked. Caitlin was a quite clever female but she never got the danger to go to university. Amari determined if she wanted to go he might pay her fees. It changed into about 1 in the afternoon and Amari was a chunk tired.

"I want a piece of sleep honey, experience loose to roam the belongings. If you need me you could wake me up." "Can I lay down with you?" "Are you sure?" "Yes." "Well come on then." He took her hand and led her to their bedroom. "I'm slumbering in here with you?" She noticed her suitcases. "That's what I had in mind however there are three other bedrooms you can select from and don't worry about being by myself within the residence with me, I can restrain myself."

Amari had let his hair and beard develop and he regarded the form as antique however while he took off his blouse Caitlin almost ran thru the door. Amari become flawlessly toned, his abs looked like they had been carved from rock. His arms have been described a lot so Caitlin desired them around her all the time.

"Keep searching at me like that and I will torture that

frame of yours. Come, lay with me." She moved from the wall with the super problem. She lay down on the mattress and Amari lay after her. He pulled her near and spooned her and inside minutes he changed into snoring gently. Caitlin however changed into hot. Amari had turned the a/c on but she turned into locating it tough to loosen up. Amari's frame was hard and warm and she or he felt secure. She wanted some other kiss. She slowly became in his hands and when she changed from head to head with him, she stared at the person she had just met.

She puzzled about what he appeared like without the beard and hair, she would point out it to him whilst the time became proper. She leaned ahead and kissed him softly. When he stirred she stopped. She waited till he was calm once more and he or she kissed him. Caitlin observed herself laying on her return with Amari firmly seated among her thighs.

"Hi." "Hello." "You were asleep." "Yet you decided to tease me, do you know what that means?" "That you will torture me?" "You examine fast." Amari decreased his head and kissed her. The fires ignited in his stomach. He ought to experience himself harden and he growled softly. "Make like to me Amari please." "No honey, not yet. Be affected person."

Amari ran his hands all over her frame and she or he couldn't include herself. She turned into writhing beneath him and he turned into getting tougher. He needed to put each of their fires out and he knew how. He slowly caressed Caitlin's leg and he maneuvered her to get dressed up till he felt her panties. He endured to kiss her and she turned into overall oblivion.

"Make it forestall Amari." "I will honey, I will." He eased

her panties down her legs, pulled them off, and threw them someplace. He got up and pulled her with him, he stood her up and unbuttoned her to get dressed. Her breasts were heavy and her nipples perked whilst the nippiness of the room hit her. He bent his head to take one into his mouth. Caitlin grabbed his head and pulled him into her chest. Amari may want to smell her scent, he knew she became equipped however these days were now not a day for that.

Her dress hit the floor and he lay her back on the bed. He kissed her breasts once more and made his way right down to her belly. Caitlin was trembling so awful, that Amari could not help but notice. He unfold her legs lightly and whilst he licked her, she nearly screamed his call. He persevered slowly and there has been no pretense, no lies, no cheating, she become simply taken part in all that he needed to supply her.

Amari hooked his fingers under her knees to provide himself higher get right of entry and he placed his fingers on her tummy. She quivered uncontrollably as he carried out his promised torture. "Let it cross honey." Caitlin turned into bursting, she knew she wanted something however no phrases could pop out, Amari become making her sense as if she could crumble into the mattress. Just when she idea she could not experience any greater satisfaction, something outstanding came about. Her body flushed from her middle and spread at some stage. As her orgasm took her to an area she had never even dreamed of, the tears came. Amari massaged her tummy, her fingers, and her legs, and whilst she eventually calmed down, the tears have been nonetheless flowing.

"Shhh, honey it's very well. I'm right here." He lay down

after her and pulled her into him and let her cry however she wouldn't stop. He knew something else was wrong. "Honey speak to me, did I harm you in a few manners?" "You do not want me." "What are you speaking approximately?" "I thought you were going to move all of the manners but you did... That instead." "Honey, if you only knew how a great deal wanted to take you but you are nevertheless married and until this is no longer an issue, I may not make you mine. I'm sorry if I made you suspect I failed to need you." "My experience is so silly."

"Honey, we just met, and already I understand what your flavor is like. I've by no means achieved that with any woman earlier however for some reason I accept it as true with you and I need you to believe me as nicely. I started on the wrong foot with you and I want to make it proper one way or the other. We might want to discuss some things however first, it's nearly 3 and I need you to be there while the children get home."

"Amari!" "Yes, hon." "Thank you for rescuing me." "Ah, my love I consider it was you who rescued me. Come and allow the dress and pass to meet the children." They got dressed and went out to the automobile. A van became pulling up whilst Amari opened Caitlin's door. He identified the emblem at the side. "Crap I forgot about her." "I can take a taxi lower back in case you want me to go."

"Well, I might not appear desirable sporting any of the clothes due to the fact the personal client is right here for you. She can leave the items we will see them when we get again." "Okay," Amari spoke to the fine female and he went back to the residence and permit her up to position the garments inside. When they got here again Caitlin had

closed her automobile door and changed into sitting quietly internal.
"She is stunning Doc, are you maintaining this one?" "If she will have me, she is not anything like the rest." "Oh, I can see that, she seems like a harmless lamb. Treat her properly Doc. Catch you later, I will ship you my invoice." "Bye Pen."
Amari got in and started the auto. Caitlin seemed uncomfortable. "She's just a good buddy honey, no one can compare to you." "I did not say anything." "You failed to must, it's written throughout your face." "I'm sorry, I noticed her and my concept, and well I got jealous because I don't have anything to offer you." "Is that what you watched? Or do you watch all you need to provide me is sex?" "Yes." Caitlin bowed her head.
"Honey, the pleasant conversation I have had because I became a teenager was today with you. You listen, you disagree when the need is, you are open with your emotions if coaxed and so far, I do not assume you have lied to me. Trust me after I say, you've got plenty extra to provide than intercourse."

"Thank you, I had to listen to that." "Okay here we are, do you need to go interior or live out here with me?" "I need to live right here with you, after being with you these days so intimately, I cannot bear for him to be close to me." "Oh, I understand the sensation."

Chapter Five

The college bus pulled up and Caitlin got out of the car to greet the kids. They screamed for her and rushed over for hugs and kisses. "Oh, I overlooked you a lot these days. Come take a seat with me I want to talk to you." "Is something incorrect mummy?" "Yes and no. I should depart for a while and till I get myself settled, you could come to stay with me on weekends, I may be right here every evening whilst you get off the bus but I won't be with you right here at night."

They both started to wail at an equal time as if they were a twin. Caitlin's heart was shredded. She desired to take them with her but she did not assume Amari became equipped for that duty as yet and he or she would by no means be able to win custody of children that had been now not hers by blood.

She appeared up and saw Amari observing them, she may want to see his coronary heart become breaking as well. She heard a legitimate behind her and Justin was coming via the door. "Will you reduce the caterwauling and get your butts interior." "I instructed you now not to talk to them in that manner, they are just hurting." "Ain't my fault you selected to depart them, what form of the mom are you?

"How dare you communicate to me that way? Children, I love you each by no means has neglected that, now passed inner and do your homework and I will get dinner for you." "No you may not, you don't stay right here anymore and you have no rights to MY kids." The youngsters cried even more difficult and clung to Caitlin's legs. "Momma don't leave us please!"

"I ought to hunnie bunnies but I will see you the following day while you get home k, I promise."

They shook their heads and went into the house sniffling.

"You are a bastard Justin you usually have been." She turned to stroll away and he grabbed her arm. Now that was a mistake. Caitlin did not have time to inform him to permit her to cross before Amari punched him in the face for the second time.

"I warned you already, do now not positioned your hands on her or any female for that remember. As a count of truth, I'm taking the kids. Honey pass percent their things this minute." "Are you critical?" Caitlin's eyes lit up the whole porch. "Yes I am, now pass, I may have a communication along with your husband."

Caitlin rushed into the children's bedrooms and started out flinging matters into bags and containers The youngsters helped too. When they went again, Justin changed into sitting in a chair smiling and Amari changed into standing by way of the door ready.

The children rushed out of the house and stood next to the automobile without even pronouncing excellent bye to their father. Caitlin just shook her head at him and walked past. Amari took a number of the matters from her and took them out to the auto. He opened the trunk and put the matters in. The youngsters were smiling at him. He smiled lower back.

"Are you going to be our new daddy?" "Would you want

that?" They each shook their heads. Amari laughed and took the relaxation of the things from Caitlin. They all got into the automobile and drove away. "How much?" "Half of the unique." "I'm sorry Amari, I appear to come with now not only baggage but a large charge tag." She whispered.

"I did not pay for you, I paid for his ignorance and they are not luggage, simply harmless bystanders. We will need to exchange around some things at home." "I didn't think about that. Are you virtually sure you need to try this?"

"In all my years the handiest aspect I became ever sure of changed into that I wanted to be a health practitioner and now I can correctly say sure I am positive about this. Are you?"

"No. I think you have taken on a lot. How do we pass forward when Justin has the upper hand?" "I have an outstanding attorney and Justin has a high-quality need for cash." "Are you leaving papa?" "Yes I am honey, do you want to go lower back?" Caitlin mentally crossed her arms. "NO MAMA! Don't make us!" "Shhhh it is okay, I may not make you. We are almost home, now be for your quality behavior." "Yes, mama."

"Last threat to returned out Amari, you may have a geared up-made family to your hands as of now." "Never, I know what I am getting into. Here we're." "Is this our domestic now mama?"

"If Amari may have us yes." "Okay."

Amari was given out and opened the door for Caitlin, then she opened the door for the children who have been already starry-eyed at the massive house. Amari opened the door for them and they slowly crept in. "I will pass get their stuff, be proper back." He kisses her on her forehead

and is going back to the auto. When he comes lower back the kids and Caitlin are waiting for him.
"I'm going to need a brand new automobile for you and the children." "I cannot force."
"That's why they have riding schools honey." Amari smiled and Caitlin smiled back. "Amari dropped down on one knee in the front of the kids. "Would you like to pick out the room you will be drowsing in?"
"Yes please." Two five-year-old voices chimed in. He held out both hands and each infant took one. He winked at Caitlin and left with the kids. Five minutes later she ought to hear screaming and laughter. She ran upstairs to discover the kids beating Amari with pillows.
"Oh my goodness." "Oh hello, we have been simply ...." A pillow to the top. He pretended to fall over. "Children!" "Yes, mama!" "Time to easy up for dinner. Tell Dr. Camden thanks for the room." "Thank you for the room, Dr. Camden." "Most welcome, I will see you in a chunk. Do you observe you could take your matters out and p.c? them into the drawers in your personal?"
"YES SIR!" Two happy voices yelled. "Well k then, I will come to get you for dinner." He and Caitlin left the two children and stood outdoor the bedroom door and listened. The kids have been speaking. "I like him, don't you?" "Yes, and he smiles at mama a lot." "She smiles at him too, I by no means saw her smile at papa and I bet Dr. Camden will by no means hit mama or us."
With that declaration, Caitlin fled after Amari. He discovered her within the kitchen hunched over the counter. He walked as much as her, pulled her up, and put his palms around her. "I am so sorry honey, I promise I would by no means hurt you or the children ever." "I took

it for them, he hates them Amari, and how should you hate your flesh and blood. He could come home drunk and go into their rooms and try and beat them and I could continually get within the manner. I couldn't permit him to contact them so I took it."

"Jesus, if he comes near them again I swear I will kill him. Neither of you is to go lower back to that residence without me, understand?" She nodded through her tears. Just then they heard the kids coming. Catherine and Joshua took one look at their mom and flew right into a panic. "Mama, what's incorrect?" "Oh you guys, I'm so that happy I have you ever with me that's all. Did you place away from all your matters?"

"Yes mama but we want a toy field big sufficient for all our toys and an e-book shelf for our books." "That's an activity for this weekend, we will go shopping if you want and you may select what you need." "We can? We have by no means been shopping earlier than." "Well, that settles that. Now, what might you like for dinner." "Pasketti and meatballs please." "Coming proper up." Caitlin looked at Amari and mouthed 'thanks'.

Chapter Six

Caitlin started dinner and the kids helped whilst Amari watched in awe. He by no means notion he might locate this sort of happiness and three instances over too. The kids have properly behaved and their grammar was impeccable. Catherine laid the desk and Joshua became trying to pour the drinks when he spilled some on the table cloth.

"Uh oh, I'm sorry mama, I didn't suggest to." Joshua positioned down the jug and ran away crying. Amari was given up and ran after him whilst Caitlin and Catherine wiped clean up and finish serving.

"Joshua?" "Yes Dr. Camden." He sniffed out from the other side of his mattress. "What's wrong?" "I spilled drink, papa hit me the ultimate time I spilled drink." "Joshua?" "Yes Dr. Camden." "Do I sound disappointed to you?" "No Dr. Camden." "Did you spill the drink on purpose?" "No! I become looking to be helpful like mama taught us, I didn't mean to." He started crying again. "Well, then it's quite ok. I spilled a drink on occasion too." "You do?" He peeked out from behind the bed. "Yes, and I needed to spill lots of drink before I got it proper." "So you aren't mad at me?" "Not in any respect. So, come permit's move get dinner, the women need to be watching for us."

Joshua stuck his head properly out, wiped his face with the

lower back of his hand, and got here out. He went through the bedroom door and Amari accompanied with a grin on his face. When they got to the kitchen Caitlin become simply placed greater ice at the table. Catherine set down the spaghetti and meatballs. Everyone sat down at the breakfast table because it seated four. "Can we are saying, grace mama?"

"Sure pumpkin."

"Dear God, thanks for sending us Dr..... Dr....." "Camden". Joshua whispered.

"Dr. Camden, I assume he's a pleasant man to permit all three of us into his home. Thank you for making mama smile once more and even though she isn't our bio... Bio...." "Biological." "Biological mom, she is the quality. Thank you for the food and the palms that organized it, especially ours. Amen."

Amari's heart was bursting with love but when he looked at Caitlin she changed into staring at the children. "Catherine?" "Yes, mama?" "Who informed you that I wasn't your mom?" "Papa did. You have been outdoor inside the lawn and we had been playing and he was drunk again. He seemed out and stated you were not our actual mother and that our real mothers didn't need us and that you might aba.....Aba....."

"Abandon," Joshua whispered. "Abandon us too. Will you mama?" "Never, Cat. As long as I have breath in my frame I will by no means depart you k." "Yes, mama." "Come now the food is getting cold and I'm certain Dr. Camden doesn't want to pay attention to any extra of our sob stories. She checked out Amari apologetically. He smiled and collected the bowl of pasta.

Everyone ate and talked and laughed and then it became

time for the youngsters to get to bed. With the whole lot that took place that day, it didn't flip out too badly. They had a new home, a new father parent and hopefully, they might regulate properly to Amari." "Papa are you able to examine us?" Joshua asked Amari. "Is that ok?" He requested Caitlin. "Go right ahead, I will pass wash up."
Amari sat within the middle of the mattress with Joshua on one side and Catherin on the alternative. They snuggled up to him as he examine their favorite ebook. Zana and the Amoeba by using Aisha King
Before Amari reached the second page they had been each out bloodless. He eased downward and slid off the bed, then placed pillows on the ends and protected them up. He put on a nighttime light and closed the door. When he got to the kitchen Caitlin became just putting the last of the dishes away and the kitchen turned spotless and the leftovers were already in the fridge.
"I ought to get used to this Caitlin." "What?" "Coming home to a spouse and loving kids. I in no way idea I could get a lot of joy out of analyzing a children's e-book and once I kissed them goodnight, Joshua whispered goodnight papa." "Welcome to my global. It feels extraordinary if you have impacted a baby's life so much that they see most effective the coolest in you. Pity Justin by no means figured that out."
"Come right here." He sat down and held out his hand. Caitlin took it and sat on his lap. "Tomorrow, I want you to report for divorce. I also need us to get married in six months and legally adopt the children but only if that is what you want as properly."
"Three months, I'm not taking the threat you exchange your mind. I want to speak to the youngsters, whatever we

do impact them." "Agreed. I want you to understand something although. I have to name the alternative ladies I have been concerned with and inform them I am finished. I am not positive how they will take it and what they'll attempt to do. I don't care approximately my recognition however now that I even have the three of you, I need to shield you from whatever else."

"Do you think you could ever love me, Amari?" "Haven't you observed? I already do. My mother taught me that loving a person is the maximum herbal factor that can show up to two humans and there's honestly no time restriction on love. I need so much to present you the whole lot you want in life and with the children, I can see I may be a happy guy, and if extra come then so be it. I may additionally need to head again to medical work however for now I just want to shop for more homes and steady my circle of relatives."

"I love the manner you observed, and I love which you encompass me to your decisions as well, please don't ever alternate the manner you're." "If I do I have you to convey me again in line. For tonight I think you should sleep in the other bedroom, children are impressionable and they may not recognize." "Okay." Caitlin sounded disappointed.

"In time my love in time." Amari studies her like an e-book. Always in song to what she was feeling or questioning. They closed up the residence left on a small light and went to their separate rooms. Around three in the morning, Caitlin changed into awoken by a toddler screaming. She flung off the covers and ran immediately to the kid's room. Catherine was thrashing about the mattress and Joshua became on the floor as though he had fallen off.

Caitlin ran to Catherine and picked her up. Amari came in as she sat down on the mattress.

"Shhhhhhhhh mama's right here infant, do not be afraid, I'm here shhh." "Josh are you okay?" Amari spoke softly.

"I'm okay papa, Cat changed into having a terrible dream and she knocked me off the bed." Amari walked over and picked him up and sat next to Caitlin. He put his arm around her. "Is she ok?" "I'm fine now papa, it become a dream it is all." "Want to tell me about it?" Caitlin whispered.

"We were playing outdoor and Justin came and took us away." Amari marveled at their adjustment of calling him papa and their actual father via his call. "He is not going to harm you, sweetie." "I understand but it became so actual." "I apprehend. Would you want to come to sleep with us for now?"

"Okay, can Josh come too? Sorry I knocked you off the bed Josh." Josh nodded his reputation of her apology.

"Sure sweetie." He checked out Caitlin and he or she turned into smiling extensively. They all went to the master bedroom and lay down on the bed, children in the center and adults on the ends. When the kids have been settled Josh spoke.

"Mama?" "Yes, candy pea." "Did you and papa have an issue?" "No Josh why could you ask that?" "When I exceeded the opposite bedroom, it wasn't made up and there may be nobody else in the house so you needed to be napping in there."

"Oh my!" "Did we cause a hassle by being right here?" Catherine requested. "Oh my goodness, the two of you are something else. Papa and I are nevertheless gaining knowledge of every other and I am still married to Justin. Until we get married we might not be napping within the same bed k?"

"Well get married the following day then." Josh yawned and fell fast asleep. "Yes mama, get married the next day then." Catherine accompanied fit. Amari attempted to stifle his laughter a lot his eyes have been watering. Caitlin gave him a glance at what you did face. She reached out her hand and he took it, they rested them on the kids and fell asleep. Amari woke up to the aroma of porridge, scrambled eggs, and toast. He got up, brushed his enamel, and went down to the kitchen.

"Morning Amari." "Morning Papa." "Morning you three, wow this looks yummy." "I did the toast." Josh piped in. "I laid the desk. Mama did the whole lot else we are not allowed to use the range but." Catherine offered.

Amari sat down and waited for Caitlin to take a seat as nicely. "Oh gosh, I forgot the bus. I have to name the provider and inform them the kids gained be there anymore for choose-up." "I can take them." "Yay, we get to trip in an automobile to school mama." "Yes you do, now devour up and cross easy up and get dressed, you do not want to be overdue."

Everyone was given equipped and Caitlin went to the spare room to pick out something from the objects the non-public client delivered. She chose a pastel inexperienced halter pinnacle and short white pants. She failed to even understand Amari has requested shoes, baggage, and different accessories as properly but she did not need to overdo it so she picked out a couple of wedge sandals and bags to match. She continually wore the locket her mother gave her and that became it.

"Mama your appearance is sweet," Josh said. "Yes, you do Caitlin. Didn't you locate any jewelry you preferred?" "I did not want to overdo it, Amari, I'm now not conversant in this." "It's okay I understand, come guys allow us to get you off to high school, your mom and I have a few things to take care of today."
They all piled into the auto and earlier than they pulled off Amari plugged his cell into the auto. When the display screen got here up he swung the engine. While driving down the road, Amari touched a velocity dial variety and the cellphone become on loudspeaker. "Nassco Limited can I assist?" "Hi Jenna Dr. Camden right here, I'd like my family car, what do you advise?" "How many Dr. Camden?" "For now there are four people, two adults, and children however it will be for a female and kids maximum of the time." "I advise the Fortuner Sir. Would you like to be available in and spot one nowadays?" "We might be there in half an hour." "I could be here sir." "Thank you."
He ended the call and touched some other range. "Hey Cam, what's up?" "We are coming to peer you in an hour David." "Walk properly in pal." Amari ended the decision. He touched some other quantity. "Camden Clinic, Sonia talking." "Hey Sonia, Dr. Camden here, do you've got any appointment slots open these days?" "Yes, Doc we've got one at noon and some other one at 1:00." "We will take the 1:00. See you then."
Amari disconnected and requested Caitlin to dial the range for the bus provider. "Barbados Transport Board School Bus Service can I help?" "Good morning that is Dr. Camden, just informing you that the Forde kids won't want the bus anymore." "I'm sorry sir however Mrs.

Forde is the simplest member of the family cleared to make that choice, I ought to touch her." "It's okay Shanice, they may be with me." "Oh sorry, Mrs. Forde." "That's ok. Have a terrific day." "You as well."
Amari ended the call. "Okay men, I could be taking you to high school any further and choosing you up as properly, is that ok?" "Yes, papa."

Chapter Seven

Amari pulled up outside the college and all of them were given out. People stared at the auto and the folks who were given out of it. Those who knew the Forde knew who Caitlin became and the reality that she got out of a highly-priced vehicle with a man who changed into not her husband, started tongues wagging, specifically one specific girl who knew what the best medical doctor looked like bare.

"So it is why he broke it off. For a young whinge, properly we can see how she likes it once I inform her what the medical doctor has been as much as."

Amari kissed the kids goodbye while preserving Caitlin's hand. When they have been correctly inside they went back to the auto, were given in, and drove off. He did not even pay any interest to the people observing them, he changed into happy and nothing else mattered.

"Caitlin, we ought to move to select out a car, then to the attorney's workplace, to the medical institution, and anything you want to do after that we can." "I'm too excited to think, I've by no means seen the youngsters so satisfied and it's because of you. Oh, why could not I have met you years in the past?" "The children needed you and years ago I could now not have been geared up for you and we may not have worked out but we're right here now and we can make our quality efforts." "Agreed."

"I need you to move again to high school. You can have a look at it in the daytime and be domestic for the children." "What approximately you?" "Me? I do not understand." "Everything has been all about me and the youngsters to this point since we met. What do you need from us, Amari?" "Love, consider friendship, interest, care, foot rubs, again rubs, holidays on the East Coast. I need the whole lot you want and I want what the kids need. That's own family for me, people sacrificing for every different."

"I suppose we will manage that." "Okay, here we are, now permit's move to choose out a vehicle."

Amari allow Caitlin to pick out what color she desired for the reason that the car could be hers whilst she was given her license. The automobile could be added later that nighttime. He would promote him and use the brand new one.

They arrived at the legal professional's office approximately fifteen minutes later. "Good morning David, this is Caitlin Forde." "Well hey Caitlin, now it makes the experience." "What makes experience?" "Amari does all his commercial enterprise with me over the smartphone, this ought to be important for him to expose up and with a beautiful female in hand."

"I am positive Amari has his motives, I have come to recognize he is very adept in his decisions.' "Wow, a girl with a perceptive brain. So, tell me, what services can I provide for you two nowadays?"

"Caitlin and I met the day before today after I went to speak to her and her husband approximately rebuilding their house which I just sold and going from hire to personal. I admit after I noticed her I modified my motive for being there and her husband regarded to sense what I had in my thoughts. I paid him three hundred and fifty thousand dollars for her to depart with me. They have two small kids who aren't Caitlin's biologically or even after six years they have no longer consummated their marriage. The children are now residing with me. I realize that is unexpected however we're positive this is a good aspect regardless of the way it got here to be. Caitlin needs a divorce, we plan to get married and legally adopt the kids."

"Wow."

"Yeah, we know." Amari reached out and took Caitlin's hand and winked at her. She blushed. "Okay, since there was no consummation, this must be a piece of cake divorce-wise. If he took the money for her to leave I am advantageous he will need greater. The difficulty of the children may be a notable project. He will want cash for them as well. Whatever you do, do no longer keep them far from him, even if you take them to the house and sit and watch him."

"He is an abusive guy, he has been beating Caitlin for years, he comes home under the influence of alcohol and when he attempts to take it out on the children she steps in. They didn't even say goodbye to him when we had been leaving. I cannot allow them to move lower back there."

"Sorry pal, they're more his kids than hers. Let's start the divorce court cases and then we can address the adoption. When do you intend to get married?" "The kids stated these days however I turned into thinking greater like six months, so one can supply us some time to get to recognize every other higher and permit the children to adjust."

"Okay, Caitlin, you have been very quiet." "Sir, I've come to consider Amari, and although I agree that his first choice was a bad one, I was a tens of millions of instances happier within the ultimate twenty-four hours than my complete life. He cannot need me for my money for the reason that I haven't any and ...."

"Ah ok I apprehend, if I know the good medical doctor here, he wants to wait till you are divorced."

"Yes."

"Okay permit me to get some facts from you and I will have the papers to signal within the week. I endorse you not telling the youngsters you plan to adopt them legally. Try not to swing them towards their father."

"Sir, my children are very smart for their age, and they have determined that once a couple of minutes of meeting him, they need Amari as their father. I had no impact over that and if we have to visit court docket they will tell us to choose what they want with no people interfering."

"I see. Okay. I will see what I can discover about your husband and decide wherein we pass from right here." She squeezed Amari's hand and smiled. An hour later, they left David's workplace and went to the hospital.

Caitlin became examined with the aid of Dr. Joseph and the best thing about Camden hospital is that every piece of a device recognized by the clinical industry will be determined there. She was given a complete checkup. She was sitting in the seek advice from the room when Amari came in and sat down.

"I can pass again out in case you need to speak to Ryan by myself." "No, I don't thoughts." She smiled at him. Just then Dr. Joseph came in. "Caitlin, I want to run some different assessments on you, I observed a boom on certainly one of your ovaries." She squeezed Amari's hand.

"Will I be capable of having children?" "You will need to attempt the first sweetie, I recognize you are nevertheless a virgin." "Sir, Amari and I just met and already he has taken on my entire own family. The children are each five years old, I cannot simply determine to attempt for a child. I need to discuss this with him first. Is there something else wrong with me?"

"No all of your organs are healthy, the consequences from the blood tests could be returned in some days. In the interim, I need you to take a regimen of vitamins and eat healthily, the tumor may go away on its personal without me having to operate." He handed her a few records. "Anything else Ryan?"

"No boss, I will let you know whilst the check outcomes come lower back." "Thanks. Come on honey, allow' us to cross." He stood up and waited for her to arise. They left the health facility and Caitlin become extraordinarily silent. "It may be okay honey, strive no longer to fear. What might you like to do next, before we pass to get the children from college?"

"Make love to me Amari." "Honey, I recognize you are scared but allow us no longer to rush this, we have so much stacked towards us and I need to be focused and this could sound ordinary but the fact that you are nevertheless a virgin works in our favor in two ways. Justin can't say he consummated the marriage and he cannot say you had been untrue on your marriage."

"I don't care, Amari, do you have any concept of what it looks like now not to be touched? To lay in bed and pain for someone to expose you to their love?" "Yes honey I do recognize however if we are to be collected and have the kids with us, we want to do this properly, you said you relied on me, don't give up on me but." "It's difficult." "So am I." "Amari!" "Sorry, you walked into that one." "Gosh." "We could have fun without going all of the manner, till then just be patient and we can get thru this." "Okay, are we able to pass and get a few ice cream? Wait no I cannot do that without the youngsters. I need to get a few garments for them, they may be developing speedy." "Not a trouble, I ought to installation an account for you so that you have money without asking me."

"What I need is a task Amari, you may be wealthy but I need my freedom, I don't mind you taking care of us, however, I need a way to move into a store and purchase a gift for you or the youngsters or maybe myself with my cash." "I can recognize that. Tell you what. I will turn one of the properties over to you to run, virtually no. I have an empty construction, I need you to take a look at it and tell me what you will do with it and I get it performed and flip it over to you, it will be your obligation after that. I am here in case you need steerage but the very last say might be yours. That way you ought not to go through making use of each person and you could nevertheless be loose to go to high school and take off your own family."

"Oh thank you this means a lot to me I might not let you down I promise." "Great, we can cross see the building now."

Chapter Eight

They pull as much as a lovable construction and right away, Caitlin can see what she wants to do. "A mall would be perfect, I saw the simplest store on the way here. There is sufficient area for offices as properly or even a cinema. What do you watch?" Amari stared at Caitlin.

"I'm sorry you do not like the concept?" "Hold on a second." Amari let her hand pass and went to the car, while his lower back had ground plans in his hand. "Oh my. You already knew what you wanted to do?" "Yes but now I do not must fear about converting a factor. I will get David to turn the property over to you."

"Wait now not but, after we are married." "Why wait?" "I don't need humans to think I'm in this for the cash. Yes, I would like to be handled properly and be capable of managing to pay for excellent things however you hardly ever realize me and you preserve blowing my world away together with your generosity."

"This is why I need you in my existence honey, you are so selfless and giving. Even if we don't emerge as together, I need this for you so you do not emerge in the same scenario as with Justin that you can't get out of and you'll be able to offer for the children to your personal."

"Thank you, Amari. How soon can we begin?" "If you can come up with an advertising plan in a few days, we can begin advertising next week. The construction is entire just ready to be rented. Retain the cinema and lease the whole thing else. I will provide you with a cellular cellphone and I will install an office for you at domestic. The rentals are already organized."

"I'm so excited, wait till the kids pay attention to this. Can I name the Mall after them?" "It could be yours to do whatever you desire. What will you call it?" Caitlin's concept for a minute. "Deejays." "Great, I get the specifications for the cinema and we can start unfashionable fitting within a month."

Amari looked up, clouds were looming. "Come on hone earlier than we get wet." "I already am." "Caitlin......" "I'm sorry, I've never said something like that earlier than." She felt ashamed. "Honey, that simple statement has me so difficult proper now I could take you in the automobile." "Oh." "Yeah oh. Let's go get the children."

When they got to the school, they noticed every other child but Justin and Catherine. They asked some humans however no person noticed the children. They went into the college to the body of workers' room. "Mrs. Forde, how are you?" One of the kid's instructors asked. "Well no longer too proper in the meanwhile, we have not seen the kids come out."

"Your 'husband' got here to get them just after lunch, he said they had a physician's appointment and you must have forgotten approximately it." Amari may want to pay attention to the venom within the teacher's voice and he became about to present her with a few of his thoughts when Caitlin fainted. "Caitlin honey, wake up for me." He rubbed her fingers, massaged her returned, and even kissed her. She stirred a piece after which she opened her eyes.

"Oh God, Justin has the kids." She attempted to rise quickly and nearly fainted again. Amari held onto her and made her sit down. "I've already called the police but they cannot do something on account that he is their organic father. Come, permit's move lower back to the residence and spot if he has them there."

"Maybe if she hadn't left them, her 'husband' would have had to take them." "Maybe in case you didn't sleep with strangers for money, you'll recognize that Caitlin is a high-quality woman and mother, I can't say the equal for you, Sophia. Have a great day." Amari lifted Caitlin and walked quickly to the auto. He opened her door and helped her in. He was given in and sat down.

"I'm sorry Caitlin." "For what Amari? For blurting out that one of the kid's instructors is a fling of yours? It's now not an issue." "It is for me and now that you realize I'm wondering in case you do not want to be with me anymore and if it truly is the case I recognize."

"You had been sincere from the beginning Amari but she just verbally attacked me not because she had proof that we are collectively but because she realized why you left her. Is this what I will undergo whilst people begin realizing, I stay in your home?"

"I'm no longer certain honey however like I said you are not a prisoner however I won't assist you to move lower back to Justin." Amari started the engine and drove inside the direction of the Forde residence. When they were given there Caitlin knew it became a waste of time. If the children have been there, they could be out of the house screaming for her.

"Stay here."

The residence appeared abandoned. Amari was given out and walked to the front door and without tons of effort, he kicked the door in. He recognize Justin took whatever he ought to and left with the youngsters. He went lower back to the car and got in. He pulled up the telephone book and looked for the radio station.

"Starcom Network can I help you? "My two kids were taken from college. I am putting out a five hundred thousand dollar praise for all of us who present information that leads to them being observed. Their names are Catherine and Joshua Forde." "I'm, sorry sir, I may have shipped the statistics to my manager and I'm sure he'll air it as quickly as we can. Do you have a number wherein I can touch you?"

Amari rattled off his cellular telephone range and his call, stated thank you, and hung up. Five minutes his mobile phone rang. "Amari?" "Hey, Andrew." "You have no youngsters, what's happening?" Amari gave him the short model of the previous few days. "Jesus, I will do what I can and I hope we will bring them home effectively. I will call if we hear something.

"Thanks." Amari hung up. "Exactly how much money do you have Amari?" For the primary time considering they determined approximately the children, Amari laughed. "Well in keeping with my banker, I have approximately eighteen million dollars in cash, stocks, bonds, and different investments. My properties are presently valued at about $three million except our residence. The health center is well worth approximately $3.5 in annual sales, the device, and the property."

"Wow." "It hasn't all been roses for me, honey, my mom gave me a good start from her life and I vowed by no means to emerge as in that role and now that I have you ever if I still have you ever, I intend to make certain you do not either." Just then his cellular phone rang. "Hello." "Papa?" "Catherine? I'm putting you on speaker telephone, mama is right here with me." "Where are you, Catherine?" "At the Coco........Coco........" "Coconut," Josh whispered. "Coconut Court Hotel. Room 28. Can you return get us to please?" "We will be there in five minutes." "Okay, papa."

Chapter Nine

Amari hung up and became the automobile round and stepped on the gas. They pulled up to the hotel, parked, and ran internally. When they were given to reception, they asked the clerk to call the police, two youngsters have been being held against their will in room 28. "Those two brats? They were screaming down the complete vicinity their father had to spank one in every one of them."

Caitlin was livid.

"If you ever call my kids brats again I will punch you within the face, now name the police and give me the damned room key." The clerk turned shocked at Caitlin's anger. She surpassed the important thing and dialed the quantity of the police station. Amari changed in advance of her and once they got to the room, he unlocked it and went internal.

"Josh, Catherine!" "Mama, Papa." They came going for walks from the bedroom. "We need to pass now, papa says he might be back, he has to name you for ran... Ran..." "Ransom;" Josh whispered. "Ransom." "Okay allow us to go, the police are on their manner." Caitlin picked up Catherine and Amari picked up Josh and rushed out of the room. They were given as a long way as the reception table, while Justin came strolling into the foyer door. Amari placed Josh down and drove them to the back of the counter. "Stay there." "Well properly…., if it isn't the

coolest physician, his slut and their bastards."
"What do you need Justin, haven't you induced sufficient trouble? The cops are on their way.' Justin pulled out a gun and pointed it at Amari. People started screaming and strolling. Amari stood there unflinching. "Take your pick out, I take the kids or my spouse." "Not taking place. You bought them don't forget!" "That money is already gone. Make them well worth my while."
"Not any other cent, Caitlin is divorcing you and the children may be followed legally via us." "Oh no, I am no longer signing something, you'll guide me so long as they may be alive." "Are you absolutely crazy?" "Oh, I am as sane as the next guy. I did a few digging on your Doctor Camden and you haven't been as upstanding as you'll have Caitlin agree with. Do you want me to inform her you've got been slumbering with other guys' better halves and that your mom turned into a prostitute for five years?"
"I already know all of that Justin, Amari isn't like you and you are not getting any greater of his money. Just go right into a nook and die." "Well somebody's coming with me these days so take your pick out." "I'll move, you live with the children." "No Caitlin, he'll kill you in case you go."
"It is ok, I'm so glad you came into my existence, Dr. Camden. I love you." She whispered into his ear.
"Mama, don't depart us, you promised." They screamed from behind the counter. "I'm no longer leaving you, I'm just going with papa to speak ok! Amari will stay with you until I get back." The children started to cry very loudly. Caitlin's coronary heart broke. She knew the instant Justin changed into able to, he might kill her but if he took the children she would by no means forgive herself. She walked over to Justin, who grabbed her and positioned the

gun to her head.

Just then the police confirmed up and aimed the weapons at Justin. "If you return any closer, I will kill her. Now let me pass." They sponsored away and allowed him to pass. He made his manner with Caitlin and shoved her into the auto and drove away. The cops observed near behind and it changed into a high pace chase. Amari wanted to leave the youngsters and pass after Caitlin but they wouldn't let him go.

"He's going to kill her Papa, he stated he knew she might go with him to keep us. Don't move he'll kill you too!" "Oh, God!" The clerk exclaimed. "Okay, I will stay with you are you hungry?" "Yes, papa." He grew to become the clerk who became now in tears on the complete scene. "Can you give them what they need and charge it to my card please?"

"I pay for something they need Dr. Camden, it is the least I could do for calling them brats."

"Thank you." "Come on kids permit's pass locate you some meals." "Are you coming Papa?" "Of course, let's move." They went to the eating place and sat down, the kids ordered burgers and fries and a juice. They also ordered cheesecake while their mom got it again and a Caesar fowl salad for Amari.

"How do you understand what to reserve from a menu?" The clerk requested. "Some of this stuff mama makes at home if she gets extra cash from the garden sales. Hers tastes better." The clerk laughed. "I'm positive it does, now consume up, and while your mom receives again you may need your electricity to provide her hugs and kisses."

"Thank you and we're sorry we made so much noise when we came in." "That is quite an okay sweetie and I'm sorry I didn't believe you." She ruffled Joshua's hair and left. They waited and waited and waited without a word. They left the eating place and went to the reception front room and sat down. The children had fallen asleep on Amari's lap.

Amari saved his eye on the door manner. When he saw her he woke the youngsters. "Look who's right here." "MAMA!" They screamed and ran over to her. "Oh my infants, I'm here. See I informed you I could come lower back. Have you been behaving?" "Yes mama, the clerk apo… apo…." "Apologized," Joshua whispered.

"Apologized and gave us food and we ordered cheesecake for you, you may choose it up before we go away." "Oh, you are so thoughtful. Are you k? Did Justin harm you?" "No mama, he hit Joshua on his palms however we're nice. I suppose papa desires a hug and a kiss so we may not hog all of your time." They let her move and went again to take a seat down."

"Hi." "Caitlin...." "Yes." "You said you cherished me." "I do." "I love you too. I don't suggest rushing you and you can inform me what came about at the manner domestic but I need to get us out of right here. Children go get your mama's cheesecake." Just then the clerk came up. "I wanted to apologies for my comment earlier, I shouldn't have judged the youngsters without knowing what become going on."

"Understood, thanks, and thank you for taking care of my circle of relatives." The children got here returned and they all left to go domestic. They have been so worn out they failed to devour any dinner, Amari took Josh and Caitlin took Catherine for his or her baths. In no time they had been out cold. "Talk to me honey, I know you failed

to need to say something with the youngsters here."
"I need a shower, include me." They went into the bedroom and headed for the bath. They stripped and stepped in. It wasn't a romantic shower, simply something to take the edge off. They completed and came out. Amari dried Caitlin's pores and skin and she or he dried his. He put on a couple of boxers and she put on a night blouse.
"When Justin drove away all I ought to consider become you and the children and that I may also in no way see you once more. I couldn't handle that. Justin isn't an excellent driving force and he couldn't manipulate the car at the speed he turned into going at. You" know whilst you see things in movies you constantly need to attempt them? I realized his seat belt wasn't on and the car he rented had dual air luggage. I waited for the right time and I grabbed the wheel and pushed it to his aspect and pulled the handbrake. The vehicle slid and crashed head-on right into a pole. My bag came out, he didn't and he went thru the windscreen and broke his neck. The police have been proper at the back of us so they reduce my bag and let me out. I didn't want to attend, so I asked one of the officers to convey me returned right here and they might speak to me tomorrow. I just had to see my babies and keep you in my palms again."
"It's over now honey, we are able to begin our lives without a fuss. I love you so Caitlin." "I love you too Amari. We nonetheless have a problem to find out although." "What's that?" "The kid's mothers are nonetheless alive, they will be contacted while the adoption software is made." "I am positive they won't show up and in the event that they do, the youngsters will need to live

with us but I will permit David to understand." "Thank you."

"Amari?" "Yes, honey." "Please." "Caitlin..........." "We almost lost every different these days, I need to feel you. Please." Amari heard the need in her voice and decided wedding be damned. He crawled over her and kissed her deeply. She moaned softly. Amari made love to her for hours and after they eventually have been satiated, they cuddled up and fell asleep in every other's palms.

Chapter Ten

The next morning become no school and Amari had promised the children he might take them shopping for clothes, e-book shelves, and a toy box. So around seven whilst he and Caitlin have been nonetheless wrapped up, the children came bouncing into the room. "Mama, papa awaken it is Saturday," Josh shouted.

"Can you hear voices, Caitlin?" "I can pay attention to yours." "Go returned to sleep then, I have to be hearing things." "Noooooo, you going to awaken, we ought to get breakfast and go shopping." "Caitlin I keep hearing voices, are you certain you didn't listen to anything?" "Mmmmm"

Amari pretended to appear all over the room and just whilst the children have been about to get worried, Amari threw a pillow. They screamed with delight and jumped up into the mattress. "Good morning you." "Morning papa. Wake up, mama!" "I'm up with all the racket you three are keeping. What might you like for breakfast?" "Can we consume out these days, it is so quiet outside," Catherine said.

"If it is okay with papa, it's now not a trouble." "Of direction, it's not. Come on Josh allow me to come up with a tub." "Come Cat, I will give you yours." They were given the kids prepared and then they took their bathe collectively."

The Fortuner had arrived the preceding evening but no person turned into in any temper to even have a look at it. But this morning all of them fussed over it. They all got in and made their way over to Sheraton Mall. Amari could see the excitement and awe in the children's eyes.
"Please don't go overboard with them." "Aw come on, I've by no means executed this before, and neither have they, allow us to have some amusing please." Amari gave Caitlin the most convincing pup dog eyes she had ever seen. She laughed "Okay however just this as soon as." "Yay, come on men, allow get breakfast first then we store."
They spent the whole day shopping for new clothes, toys, and books for the kids, there has been no way they could place the matters in the SUV so Amari paid shipping fees to take the things back to the house. They placed the youngsters to bed and went down to the dwelling room. "Oh, you're spoiling them."
"I recognize however after everything they had been via they wished it and so did you. I even have something for you, Caitlin." "I don't need something else, you have given me a lot already." "Oh, this you clearly want." He got down on one knee and produced an emerald engagement ring. "Oh, Amari." "Marry me, Caitlin."
"Say sure mama." The children whispered from the doorway, "I have an idea that you had been drowsing." "We pretended so papa may want to ask you." "Sneeks." "Yes, Dr. Amari Camden I will marry you. Four years later, "Amari honey, are you taking the kids this morning?"
"Yes I am, are you going to work this morning?" "Yes best for some hours, your baby appears to have a fondness

for napping inside the nook of my stomach." "Oh, now he's my baby." "Yep, you stated it." Amari walked over and put his fingers on his spouse's six-month stomach. "Don't mind your mom, she's just suggesting, now because you are dad's baby, make mummy comfortable for me." He endured to rub and the infant regarded to reply due to the fact she or he moved once more." "I do not trust that just occurred." "I even have skills oh wife of mine." "Yeah, I suppose this is how I got pregnant to start with." "I can show you some of them now if you want." "I am sure you may Dr. Camden but we are starting in some weeks and you'll now not forestall progress." She tiptoed and kissed him on his cheek.

Amari had desired to make an alternate in his existence, so when the day of their wedding ceremony came he was given a shave and a haircut. Caitlin had in no way complained about his seems but he wanted her to be happy with him. When Caitlin stepped into the church and Amari became around, she paused at the door. It became simplest whilst he smiled she realized what he had completed. Her face beamed with happiness.

They launched Ceejays mall six months later and the kids reduce the ribbon. Since then Caitlin had completed her degree in Business Management. The kids had been doing splendid in school and with a brand new child on the manner, everybody changed into satisfied. The kid's mother came to peer them when the adoption papers had been filed and once they told the tale of ways Justin threatened them in order that they allow the kids to go with him. Caitlin definitely blew every person away.

"If you permit us to undertake the kids you may see them every time you need if that is what they want. I actually have regulations. You may also have given beginning to them however for all their lives I changed into there and that means something to them and me. You do now not make selections for them until you ask us first. You do not simply show up and take them, allow us to realize first." The ladies agreed on the grounds that then there had been no troubles.

Joshua and Catherine grew as much as be docs underneath the steerage of Amari. He grew to become the health center over of their names once they became twenty-five. Caitlin constructed her corporations with Amari's help and in the twenty years they were married, they now owned fifteen malls twenty-five, houses, and she or he ran a children's home. They had one extra infant and existence changed notably.

www.ingramcontent.com/pod-product-compliance
Lightning Source LLC
LaVergne TN
LVHW050421160726
843469LV00041B/1179

* 9 7 8 9 3 5 6 1 0 7 8 7 8 *